SPRUCE GROUSE

ING FISHER

LOON

OYSTERCATCHER

HERON

MERGANSER

Adventures in
DESOLATION
SOUND

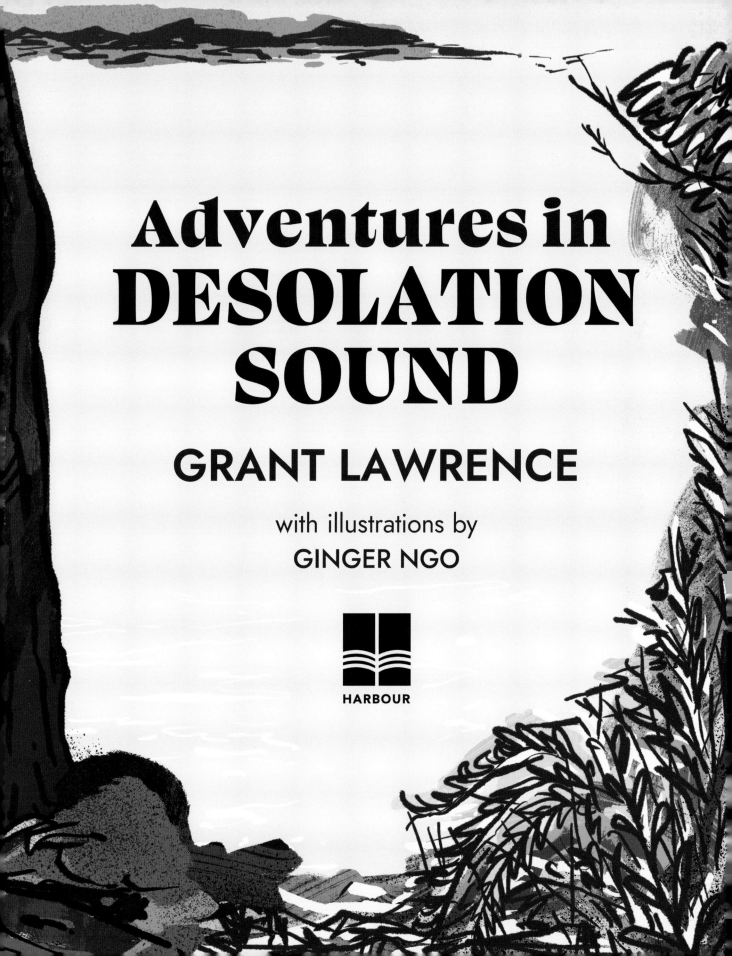

Adventures in DESOLATION SOUND

GRANT LAWRENCE

with illustrations by
GINGER NGO

HARBOUR

When my sister and I were little, we liked to stay inside and watch TV. A lot of TV. We watched TV so much that our eyes would get itchy. But we kept watching.

THE LOOOVE BOAAAT...

Our dad did not like TV. He loved outdoor wilderness adventures. He would make us turn off the TV and go outside with him. Our mom and our dog, Aggie, would come too.

These trips usually turned out to be very wet and cold, and we all had to sleep in a soggy tent that smelled like a cross between old cheese and the lost-and-found box at school. Bleh!

Dad called it

We called it

One day, Dad told us that he had come up with a solution. We thought that meant he had found a battery-powered TV for our tent. Nope. His new plan was to build us a family cabin in the wilderness, close to the ocean, in a place called Desolation Sound. Dad told us there were lots of animals there in the forest and in the ocean.

My glasses began to fog up. That's what happened when I got scared. But Dad was very excited. My mom, sister, and me not so much.

WOULD YOU BE?

"One more thing," added Dad. "There will be no TV at this cabin." My sister, Heather, started screaming. Dad shouted that the cabin would have something better than TV.

UMMM...

"W-w-w-what's better than TV?" I stammered.

"REAL LIFE!" Dad answered.

Soon it was time to make our first trip to the cabin ... and it took forever! We had to drive for an entire day and ride on two big, white 'n' rusty ferry boats.

The road between the two ferries had so many twists and turns that it made Heather barf all over the back seat like an out-of-control firehose. It was so gross it made me waterfall-barf. Then we both threw up on our mom when she tried to reach around from the front seat to clean it up. Then our dog Aggie barfed on Mom, too.

Mom shouted at Dad to stop our car. But he wouldn't! He was worried we'd miss the next ferry, so he put on a tape by The Beach Boys and kept driving. We missed the next ferry anyway.

Hours later, after many more twists and turns, Dad skidded to a stop at the end of a muddy dirt road in the forest. We parked beside an old rotten gate.

Dad told us to be really quiet. Soon we were sneaking through someone's apple orchard with all our stuff to get down to a beach.

Then we heard barking. A pack of
horrible-looking dogs burst out of
the orchard like a storm of teeth. My
glasses fogged over instantly.

WHO ARE YOU?

WHAT ARE
YOU DOING ON
MY PROPERTY?!

The old lady who owned the dogs had
grey hair that looked like my mom's knitting
wool after Aggie had chewed on it.

Dad politely explained that we were on our way to our new cabin, which was on the other side of the water, and that her beach was the best place to load up our boat.

The old lady told us that her name was Cougar Nancy, and that she had lived there her whole life. Cougars would chase her chickens and goats, so she shot at them with her rifle. Cougar Nancy became a friend of ours, and we soon liked her very much.

When Dad rowed us away from the beach, a seal popped
its head out of the ocean, right beside our boat, like a
jack-in-the-box! At first, Heather and I jumped back, afraid,
but soon we were leaning over the edge of the boat watching
the seals and jellyfish in the clear ocean water.

Finally, our boat thudded to a stop against the shoreline rocks. It was getting dark. We looked up and saw our new little cabin perched on the rocks like a giant crab.

Inside the cabin, it was cold and dark, but it didn't smell like old cheese! Or the lost-and-found box! YAY! Instead, it smelled like fresh-cut wood. Mmmmmm.

Dad lit some lanterns because there was no electricity. And there was no toilet. We had to go outside, in the dark, behind the cabin, to poo into a plastic bucket. For real.

It took us a long time to fall asleep, because Desolation Sound at night was as quiet as a math test.

"What do you think is on TV right now?" whispered my sister from her lower bunk.

"Probably *The Love Boat*," I whimpered back sadly from my top bunk.

But … the next morning was bright and sunny. On one side of the cabin, we squinted out to the ocean that sparkled like a million tiny diamonds. We spotted kayakers paddling near some islands.

On the other side, we could look right down into a little cove. The water was so clear, we could spy all sorts of amazing underwater sea creatures.

Then Dad pointed up to the sky. There were birds everywhere.

WHICH ONE IS YOUR FAVOURITE?

But then I spotted something big and hairy moving along the edge of the forest.

"D-D-D-Dad," I stammered. "Is … is … is that a bear?" My glasses were so fogged up, it was hard to tell.

"No, that's Russell," Dad answered. "He's the Hermit of Desolation Sound."

"What is a hermit?" Heather asked.

"A hermit is someone who mostly likes to be left alone," Dad explained, "but Russell is a friendly hermit. He lives in a shack down by the beach."

Russell the Hermit was a lot different than our parents, but he soon became another family friend. Russell would take us on walks in the forest, showing us yummy berries that we could pick and eat, and some plants that he said we should never touch.

Russell also took us to a lookout high above the ocean. Down below was a long and narrow bay shaped like a big lollipop. Russell told us that this was a special place called *q'aq'iq'ay* (Kahkaykay).

Not so long ago, thousands of Indigenous people from the Tla'amin, Klahoose and Homalco First Nations would gather there in a winter village along the shore to hold large feasts called Potlatches.

Heather and I gazed
down in wonder.

Every day brought a new adventure in Desolation Sound.
Russell taught us how to catch fish and dig for clams.

Sometimes, we would see Tla'amin people paddling long traditional canoes to visit their old village site.

We'd wade in the warm water of the cove with Aggie, and I even got up the nerve to try a zunga. That's a rope that's tied to a tree branch that hangs over the water like a dangling snake. From the shore, you swing out over the ocean and … let go! It was scary at first but lots of fun.

On rainy days, we'd read books, play chess with Russell or
visit Cougar Nancy for fresh-baked scones smothered in her
homemade blackberry jam.

By the end of that first summer, my glasses didn't fog up so much anymore, and we almost forgot that we even had a TV.

"Dad!" shouted Heather. "We don't need *The Love Boat*, because we love *our* boat!"

And we couldn't wait to come back for more adventures in Desolation Sound.

DEDICATED TO
THE MEMORY OF

BEV SHAW

TALEWIND BOOKS, SECHELT, BC

–G.L.

Text copyright © 2024 Grant Lawrence
Illustrations copyright © 2024 Ginger Ngo

1 2 3 4 5 — 28 27 26 25 24

Harbour Publishing Co. Ltd.
P.O. Box 219, Madeira Park, BC, V0N 2H0, www.harbourpublishing.com

Dust Jacket and text design by Ginger Ngo
Printed and bound in South Korea

Harbour Publishing acknowledges the support of the Canada Council for the Arts, the Government of Canada, and the Province of British Columbia through the BC Arts Council.

Library and Archives Canada Cataloguing in Publication
Title: Adventures in Desolation Sound / Grant Lawrence ; with illustrations by Ginger Ngo.

Names: Lawrence, Grant, 1971- author. | Ngo, Ginger, illustrator. | Adaptation of (work): Lawrence, Grant, 1971- Adventures in solitude.

Identifiers: Canadiana (print) 20240369327 | Canadiana (ebook) 20240369386 | ISBN 9781990776878 (hardcover) | ISBN 9781990776885 (EPUB)

Subjects: LCSH: Lawrence, Grant, 1971-—Childhood and youth—Juvenile literature. | LCSH: Desolation Sound (B.C.)—Biography—Anecdotes—Juvenile literature. | LCGFT: Autobiographies. | LCGFT: Picture books.

Classification: LCC FC3845.D47 L38 2024 | DDC j971.1/31—dc23

FOR MY HERMIT, TRUNG
–G.N.

THE CABIN

ME AND RUSSELL FISHING

COUGAR NANCY

RUSSELL

DAD

MOM

ME

HEATHER